THE SNOWMAN the animated film is available on Polygram video
THE SNOWMAN is a TVC London production
director DIANNE JACKSON supervising director JIMMY MURAKAMI
producer JOHN COATES executive producer IAIN HARVEY
music and lyrics by HOWARD BLAKE

Published by Ladybird Books Ltd
A Penguin Company
Penguin Books Ltd, 80 Strand, London WC2R 0RL, England
Penguin Books Australia Ltd, 250 Camberwell Road, Camberwell, Victoria 3124, Australia
Penguin Books (NZ) Ltd, Cnr Rosedale and Airborne Roads, Albany, Auckland, New Zealand

This edition published by Ladybird Books 2004
3 5 7 9 10 8 6 4
© Snowman Enterprises Ltd, 1988

Raymond Briggs'
The
Snowman ™

Ladybird

The Snowman

It was morning and as soon as
he opened his eyes and saw the
bright, white light coming
through the window,

James knew it would be a magical day...

It was **SNOWING!**

He'd never dressed
so quickly. Hardly
time for breakfast!

At *last* he was outside making
giant footprints in the snow
and throwing snowballs.

He began to roll a huge snowball and suddenly had an idea. The *best* thing to do would be to make a... SNOWMAN.

A big , big body.

A quick lunch – no time to stop!

A big round head.

Coal eyes, a tangerine nose, a hat and scarf and last of all… James drew a mouth with his finger.

His snowman was finished.

His snowman was *smiling!*

Soon it was time for bed...

but it's hard to sleep when
you're thinking of a snowman
outside, all alone.

James got up and went out into
the night. The day had been
special...

but *this* was magical.
The snowman waved,
raised his hat

and walked
towards
the house.

James took the snowman's hand
and they went indoors.

Ordinary snowmen *never* go
inside a house but *this* snowman
wanted to see
everything.

The 'fridge was best – it was cold, just how snowmen like it! Upstairs, Mum and Dad were fast asleep.

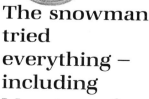

The snowman tried everything – including Mum's perfume, which nearly made him... sneeze!

The snowman danced to a music box and played with James's toys.
Mum and Dad didn't wake up.

Back outside they rode through the fields and forests on Dad's motorbike...

But the snowman needed to be cold and the motorbike made his legs very hot.

So James took the snowman to the big freezer and soon ...the snowman's legs were mended.

Then suddenly the snowman stopped smiling and listened.

What could he hear? Was he remembering something?

Then he began to run across the snow. James ran with him. He caught the snowman's hand and... all at once... they were walking in the air...

looking far below...
holding very tight...

and flying
across the
world.

When at
last
they
landed, the
snowman
led James
through dark, dark woods...

until they came upon the most amazing sight that James could ever have imagined.

All the snowmen and snow-women in the world had come for a party!

And there was Father Christmas!
He gave James a present
– and a hug.

Then they all ate
and drank and
danced and
danced…

and danced...

until it was time to go home.

They
flew
back the
same way they
had come...

and soon they landed safely in James's garden.

The snowman stood where James had first made him

but then
James ran back,
gave him
one last hug...

and
whispered
'Thank
      you'.

Next morning the sun was shining. James leapt out of bed – rushed down the stairs and out through the door to see his very special snowman.

He couldn't believe his eyes as he walked towards a heap of melted snow, and a hat, a scarf, a tangerine and some pieces of coal.

Had he been dreaming?

James felt in his dressing gown pocket and pulled out a snowman scarf – his present, given to him by Father Christmas, far away on one magical night.